Jasmin i krutrök

En kort novell om Rajesh Patel i Saigon, 1974–
en berättelse om ensamhet, begär och lojalitet
i en stad på randen till förändring

Huynh Tan Hung

april 2025

JASMINE IN GUNSMOKE

A short story about Rajesh Patel in Saigon, 1974 – a tale of loneliness, desire, and loyalty in a city on the brink of change.

Written by Huynh Tan Hung, April 2025. 50 years after the war's end.

Part I: Incense and Red Lanterns

Saigon, April 1973

Saigon lay heavy with heat and gasoline fumes as he stepped through the mother-of-pearl entrance. The chaos of the street was muffled by thick velvet curtains, and beyond them waited a different war – quieter, seductive.

The room smelled of incense, jasmine, and something else... something that couldn't be named, only felt.

She sat in the half-shadow, on a low divan draped in golden brocade. The light from red lanterns danced across her bare shoulders, glittering on the sweat beads running down her neck. Her eyes – dark as coffee and just as bitter – met his with a calm only someone used to men's gazes could possess.

"Mr. Soldier," she whispered, her voice carrying all the weariness of the war and all the promises of the night.

He sat beside her, his hands trembling slightly – not from fear, not anymore – but from something older, something he thought he had left in the jungle: desire.

Her fingers wandered across his chest, slowly, almost scientifically, as if she were mapping the scars on his skin and the stories they carried.

Their bodies met in a dance without words, where each movement was both escape and surrender, a moment's peace in a land where nothing was sacred anymore – except this.

He felt her breath against his collarbone, soft and rhythmic, like the waves against the shore in Da Nang. In the room, there was only the slow creak of the fan, the muffled hum from the courtyard, and their breaths weaving together into a new kind of music – low, swaying, almost sacred.

She leaned forward, letting her black hair sweep over his chest like a waterfall—cool and heavy. Her lips moved along his neck, not hungrily, but as if each kiss were a promise of forgetting. Her hands opened him gently, layer by layer, like an incense box from the market—each shirt button a new breath.

"You don't need to speak," she whispered. "They all say the same things anyway."

He answered her with hands, with lips. Let his fingertips trace the silken line from her neck to the small of her back, where her kimono had slipped aside. Her skin was warm, alive, like the promise of something he no longer dared believe in.

They sank into pillows and linen sheets that smelled of cedar and sweet tobacco. Outside, distant artillery rumbled, but in here there was only her body, her rhythm, her world.

He lost himself in it—let her lead, let her sound, let her take—until they were both slick with sweat, their muffled moans mingling with the thick haze of incense.

When all was still again, he lay with his head on her chest, listening to the beat of her heart. She stroked his hair as if he were a child being lulled to sleep.

"What's your name?" he whispered, despite her words.

She smiled faintly and kissed his forehead.

"Tonight, I'm whatever you need me to be."

Her body was warm and heavy against his, as if she rested with her whole soul. No masks, no lies—only breath and skin. He traced his fingertips along her back, following the soft curve of her spine down to her hip, where her kimono lay tied like a forgotten promise. The fabric whispered at his touch—thin, almost weightless—but between them, there was no cloth left to hide desire.

She moved slowly, drawing her thighs against his—a gesture more question than command. He responded with hands, with caresses that no longer fumbled but searched—recognized. There was a rhythm between them now, an understanding born only when two people let their guards down at exactly the same moment.

She turned over him, slow as a flame, and straddled him, eyes locked with his. No performance, no pretense. Just closeness. She took his hands and guided them to her breasts—let him feel their weight, their warmth, their life.

"Hold me like this," she said, barely audible, as she let her hips lower onto him in a motion so slow it felt outside of time.

They melted together there, in a dance where every movement was like waves against a shore they both thought was lost. He no longer knew where he ended and she began. Her name remained a mystery, but her body spoke a language he instinctively understood—a language without syllables, only sensation, only flesh and closeness.

She leaned down, letting her hair form a tent around their faces, the world vanishing into her scent. Jasmine, sweat, and a trace of French perfume. She kissed him deeply, with tongue, with her whole mouth, as if trying to drink him in. And he let her.

Their movements grew faster, deeper, the sounds fuller. The old bedframe creaked in protest, but neither of them heard it. When climax came, it was like a storm—silent at first, then with an inner roar, a release that made him hold tighter, breathe deeper, tremble.

They stayed like that, still in each other's grasp, wrapped in warmth and darkness.

"I haven't felt that in a long time," he said quietly.

She smiled, kissed him beneath the ear and murmured, "This is all we do here."

It had gone quiet outside—as if the whole city was holding its breath. Only the fan's whisper and their breathing filled the room. She lay on her side, back to him, and he saw how. the sweat had made the sheet stick to her skin. Slowly, he ran his hand down her back, along the smooth curve, until her breathing grew heavier.

"Again?" she whispered, as if she already knew the answer.

He leaned in, kissed her shoulder, let his tongue trail along her spine. She stretched out like a cat, exposing herself to him without a word. He gently turned her onto her back, spread her thighs, and lowered his mouth to her. This time, it wasn't tender. It wasn't careful—it was hungry. As if he wanted to devour her whole.

She clutched the sheets, let her head fall back. Her moans were muffled but unmistakable, a rhythm that built with every stroke of his tongue, every suck, every deeper pull. Her fingers tangled in his hair, pulling him closer, as if she never wanted it to end.

When she came, it was silent—but her whole body spoke what her voice did not. Tremors, shudders, a taut arch of her back that slowly melted again.

He crawled up behind her, laid a hand on her hip. She turned her head slightly, looked at him over her shoulder with a smile that was both inviting and challenging. Then she leaned forward, got on all fours, hips raised like an invitation.

"Do whatever you want now," she whispered. "I won't say no."

He took his time—caressing, teasing, preparing. She sighed as he entered her from behind, slowly, deliberately, and there was no moment of hesitation between them. Her nails tore into the sheets, his hands gripped her hips like he was holding on to something that could be lost at any moment. Every thrust was a signal, a statement, a proof that they were still alive—in the middle of a war, in the middle of loss, this moment of pure, raw intimacy existed.

When he came, it was with a quiet moan, buried deep in her neck, and they collapsed together into a heap of heat, sweat, and skin.

Afterward, they lay in silence, entangled in each other's bodies. The sweat slowly cooled on their skin, and the fan continued its eternal lament. She lay on her stomach, one arm under the pillow, the other resting on his chest, as if trying to keep him there—in the room, in the moment, in her.

But something had already begun to slip away.

He felt it in his chest first—that familiar emptiness that always came afterward. Like a deep breath that never quite filled the lungs. She didn't move, but he knew she sensed the shift. They always did.

"That was nice," she said softly. Not to comfort, not to flatter—just to say it. As if she needed to hear it herself.

He got up slowly, pulled on his trousers. Looked down at her where she lay, naked in the tangle of sheets and steaming skin. She suddenly didn't seem so mysterious anymore—just tired.

Just a woman.

He reached for his wallet. Moved toward the table where her perfume bottle stood, a lone cigarette resting in a crystal glass. He calculated the amount quickly—not too much, not too little. Placed the bills beneath the cigarette, as if that somehow refined the act itself.

"It wasn't supposed to feel like this," he said quietly.

She sat up, pulled a kimono over her shoulders, and lit the cigarette with a matchbook bearing the logo of the classic Hotel Continental. She exhaled the smoke slowly, without meeting his gaze.

"None of us controls that," she replied.

He wasn't sure if it was comfort or accusation.

As he walked toward the door, something held him at the threshold—a weight in his chest that wouldn't let go. He wanted to turn around, to say something more, something real. But the words didn't come. Just a nod, almost apologetic.

She was already back on the divan, as if nothing had happened. The red lanterns flickered across her face, but her gaze was somewhere else.

When the door clicked shut behind him, it was as if the world lost its color. The war rumbled on outside, but it was something else gnawing at him now. Something he couldn't blame on bombs, or death, or hunger.

Maybe it was just himself.

The door closed with a soft click, and then—only silence. No key turning, no chain sliding into place. Just a door that closed, and with it—another moment lost to time.

She remained on the divan, the cigarette glowing slowly between her fingers. The smoke curled upward toward the ceiling, dancing in the red glow of the lanterns, as if trying to whisper away something she didn't dare remember.

The bills lay untouched on the table. She glanced at them without reaching. Not yet. There was a line between a body and coin, and it was too soon to cross it.

She took a deep drag, held the smoke in her lungs until it burned. Not because it calmed her— but because it was something to feel. Something real.

There were so few things like that left.

Her thoughts didn't linger on him—not in that way. His name was already gone. But something had shifted inside her—not big, not dangerous, just... unfamiliar. He had held her like it meant something. Looked at her as if she were more than just a body in a room. And those were always the dangerous ones. The ones who pretended not to want more—but accidentally gave too much.

She stood up slowly, feeling it in her hips. There was an ache there now—a reminder—but she welcomed it. Pain was easier than emotion. She pulled the kimono around her, tied it with practiced hands. Walked to the window and opened it a crack.

Outside, Saigon glowed like a fever dream. Vespas, lanterns, barefoot boys darting between cars, a woman selling something from a bicycle cart. Life went on, indifferent, and she stood there—in a room scented with men, perfume, war, and loneliness.

She took the last drag, pressed the cigarette into the ashtray, and watched the ember die. Then she walked to the table, picked up the bills, folded them quietly, and placed them in the drawer beneath the vanity mirror. In the mirror, her own gaze met her. Not hard. Not tired. Just... real.

"Tonight, my name is whatever you need," she whispered to herself, like a mantra, a reminder.

And then she turned her back to the mirror, began making the bed again—for the next body, the next night, the next illusion.

Her real name was Linh.

Part II: Behind the Mountains, in the Valley Where It All Began

Da Lat, 1972

Before Saigon. Before perfume scents and velvet rooms. Before she learned to kiss without feeling, She lived in Da Lat—high in the mountains, where morning mist whispered through the pines and flowers bloomed like silent prayers to the sun.

Linh was sixteen when the war reached the villages around Da Lat. Not with bombs, not at first—but with soldiers. Men in green uniforms who spoke through interpreters, bought rice with cigarettes, and stared at her mother as if she were a piece of meat. Her father worked the fields—a quiet man with soil beneath his fingernails and grief rooted deep in his spine. Her mother sewed clothes for French women who no longer remained, but whose taste still lingered.

Linh was beautiful. She knew that. Not because anyone told her—But because the looks changed. They lingered too long. They thickened the air.

When her brother was taken into the army—conscription, they said, for the good of the nation—something broke in the house. Her mother fell silent. Her father drifted further out among the terraces, began sleeping beneath the stars.

She was seventeen when she left with a woman from the city. An older, elegant lady with red nails and a voice like the softest silk. "In Saigon, they need girls like you," she had said.

"You'll have a better life there than here. You'll smell like the flowers you grew up with."

And Linh believed her.

The first weeks in Saigon were disorienting. People everywhere, noise around the clock, heat that refused to let go. She lived in a small room above a shop, helped serve tea to French officers, scrubbed floors, was given clothes to wear—clothes she could never have afforded herself.

Then came the first night. The first man. There was no question. No gentle transition. Just a statement: this is your life now.

She didn't cry. Not then. It came later, in dreams, after he had already left.

She learned quickly. How to smile the right way. How to smell right, say the right thing—never too much, never too little. How to go from girl to illusion.

But she always kept Da Lat inside her—The scent of pine, the sound of crickets, the rain tapping on the tin roof. And in the moments when the room fell silent, when the fan's hum felt far away, she could close her eyes and feel like Linh again.

Just for a moment.

Part III: Le Papillon Noir

Saigon, August 1973

Linh had started to build a kind of double life in Saigon: one foot in the velvet of the brothel,

the other in the smoky, bourbon-scented world of music, strippers, and shadows. And there, in the crowd, a new presence began to watch her from the dark:

Linh quickly learned not to place all her nights in the same bed.

After half a year at the brothel, she heard about a place further down in the city—

Le Papillon Noir, half strip club, half jazz bar, where soldiers, smugglers, and journalists mingled with dreamers and the lost. It was a place where no one asked questions as long as you could keep the rhythm.

They were looking for a pianist for the evenings—someone who could play French chansons, old Vietnamese ballads, and the occasional Cole Porter tune without staring at the sheet music.

Linh said she could play.

It was a lie. But she learned. Quickly.

She played with fingertips that remembered melodies her mother used to hum back home in Da Lat. She played with her gaze lowered, as if she didn't know that every man in the room was watching her neck more than the keys. Some nights she wore black gloves, red on others—

always matching the light and the mood.

And it was there she saw him for the first time.

A man who sat alone in the corner closest to the stage. Indian, clearly. But not like the men in the spice shops. He wore a long shirt even in the heat. Clean-shaven, well-groomed, and eyes that never smiled. Rajesh, someone had said. A businessman. Perhaps a smuggler. Perhaps just rich enough that no one dared to ask, or a poor loner with no hope and no shame.

He came every Thursday. Always ordered the same thing: Old Fashioned, no ice. Never said a word to her. But his gaze lingered – not hungry, not like the others. More like a judge in silent retreat.

Linh soon noticed that he never looked at the strippers. Not even when they undressed in front of his table. He only looked at her. At her hands. At her shoulders. At the music that poured out of her.

One evening – when the rain poured down outside as if the sky wanted to wash away the entire city – a red orchid lay atop her piano after her set was over. No card. Just the flower.

She knew it was from him.

Part IV: Mr. Patel – An Indian in Vietnam

Saigon, October 1974.

The morning was humid as usual. Rajesh Patel sat on his balcony, leaning against the flaking iron railing, a cup of strong chai in his hand. The sounds of bicycles, shouting street vendors, and a distant explosion blended into something he had long since stopped reacting to.

He looked down toward the shop. Old Mrs. Thu was scrubbing the steps with her usual determination. She knew what she was doing – each movement was like a dance, a kind of discipline amid the chaos. She nodded politely at him. He raised his hand slightly. Their exchange was always wordless.

Inside the shop, the bolts of fabric were neatly arranged – imported cotton from Gujarat, embroidered lace from Varanasi, a bit of silk from Hanoi. It smelled of dust, incense, and tobacco. A young boy, maybe thirteen, entered with a letter.

Rajesh broke the seal slowly. It was from his mother. The handwriting was shaky but concise. She asked him to come home. "You are too old to live alone. Your cousin's daughter is ready. Her father awaits your answer."

He folded the letter without replying.

That evening, he sat at the bar at Le Papillon Noir with a half-empty bottle of French rice wine beside him. An American officer was yelling in Vietnamese-accented English in the background, but Rajesh wasn't listening. He was watching Linh, who was sitting at the piano. She wasn't playing. Just sitting there, with her hands in her lap. She had quit the bar a year ago, but still came by sometimes, as if her shadow couldn't leave the place behind. Rajesh admired her beautiful face from a distance.

When he stood up to leave, she followed him silently.

They walked through the rain, down narrow alleys. Dirty water splashed up on his trousers, but he didn't care. They said nothing. When they reached the house, he took out the key, opened the door, and let her in first.

Inside, he turned on the light.

"You can sleep here tonight," he said. "The rain's getting worse."

She nodded. Went to the room where she sometimes slept. But before she closed the door, she turned around.

"You got a letter today?"

He nodded. "From India."

"Are you going back?"

He didn't answer right away. Then:

"India feels like a book I read a long time ago. I remember the plot, but not the details."

She gave a sad smile. Closed the door.

Later that night, he sat on the balcony again. He heard distant gunfire, as always. But the scent of jasmine from the courtyard drifted into the air. He leaned back, lit a cigarette, and looked up at the stars fading in the glow of Saigon's streetlights.

And for a moment, he felt neither at home nor lost.

He simply existed.

Part V: The Silence of Rain

The relationship between Rajesh and Linh deepens, even as Saigon moves toward its fall

Saigon, March 1975.

It rained every day now. The sky hung like a gray lid over the city, and the sound of helicopters was as common as birdsong. Rajesh knew the end was near. Everyone talked about it – about the Americans and French fleeing, about what would happen when the North came.

But his world had shrunk to two rooms, a balcony, and the woman who used to arrive in silence.

Linh had started coming more often. Not just as a friend and lover, but as his beloved – she was simply there. Sometimes she brought rice, sometimes just silence. They sat across from each other and ate, like an old couple who no longer needed words.

One evening, she arrived with an envelope.

"My sister in Danang has secured a place on the boat that can take us away from here. She says there's room for me too. We can leave tomorrow night."

Rajesh looked at her, for a long time.

"We?"

"Yes. You can come with me."

He shook his head slowly. "My shop is here. My things. My life."

She gave a crooked smile. "The shop is empty. Your things are gathering dust. Life… that's me."

It was one of the few times she had said something that burned.

He walked her to the door that night. She kissed him lightly on the cheek, stroked his shaft, and took him into her mouth – deeply and tenderly.

"I'm leaving tomorrow, with or without you," she whispered.

The following day, time lost its shape. He sat in the shop, staring at fabric no one wanted anymore. The city was in chaos. People were running. The wealthy were packing. The poor were waiting.

At sunset, he went up to his room. Took out the letter from his mother. The scent of paper and incense. He thought of India. Of childhood. Of how he never truly belonged there, either.

Night fell. He stood on the balcony.

Then he got up. Put on his white shirt. The one stained with tea and rice wine. It was the only one that fit. He walked down the stairs, out into the street. Toward the harbor.

When he arrived, the boat was gone.

In the mist, he saw a lone figure by the pier. Linh.
She had waited.

They said nothing. Just took each other's hands.

And as the shadows of helicopters passed over them, they stood there. Two people without a country, without a future—but with each other.

Part VI: The Rice Field

Vietnam, April 1975 — Just outside Saigon

The earth was warm beneath their feet, damp, sticky. The rice fields lay across the land like sweaty sheets, breathing heavily in the haze of gunpowder and heat. The sky rumbled now and then – artillery from the north, replies from the south – but no one ran anymore. Everyone was waiting, either for peace or for death.

Rajesh and Linh walked silently through the field, carrying a sack of rice they would never have time to cook. She stopped suddenly.

"Why do you always stare at me from behind when you think I don't notice?" she asked.

"Because when I look at you, I forget all this."

"Then show me," she said.

It began as a whisper – A hand on her back, A dirty kiss tearing the dust from her sweet lips. Nothing soft. Nothing romantic. His hands slid beneath her tunic, gripped her hips, pulled her close in the steaming air. Rice stalks bowed around them like silent witnesses. She pressed herself against him, panting like an animal. A tremor passed through the ground – a grenade exploded a kilometer away – But still they moved, slowly, desperately.

He pushed her down into the mud. Wet fingers, torn fabric, her nails raking his back. She moaned loudly, holding nothing back. Her whole body burned – a different war, one only they knew.

"Faster," she whispered.

"You're everything," he answered.

Birds lifted in a flock farther off. The sound of gunfire faded. Now, only heartbeats remained. His body above hers. Her legs wrapped around him. Everything in motion, like the water beneath the rice. His length throbbed inside her, faster and faster, a rhythm not of war, but of survival, of two bodies refusing to vanish quietly. Their breath tangled. Mud clung to skin. The world cracked and trembled around them—but for a moment,

they were the only thing still alive.

Part VII: The Child and the Bottle

Bangkok, Summer 1975

They made it to Thailand on a cargo boat. Linh vomited the entire way, pale and dizzy, while Rajesh held her tightly around the waist, sweating and awake for days. In Bangkok, they rented a room above a billiard hall. The mattress was thin and stained. The fan didn't work. She cried often.

One evening, she sat on the floor with an empty rice packet in her hand.

"I'm late," she whispered.

He understood. First with his eyes. Then with his body—a strange mix of fear and something he didn't dare call hope.

Time passed slowly. Life was hard. They starved, and had barely any money. Linh grew quieter.

Each night she placed her hands over her belly and looked as if she already knew how it would end.

Rajesh began to drink. At first, just a little. Then every night. Whisky, preferably Scotch, sometimes cheap rice vodka. Linh said nothing. She only looked at him – with that gaze that…it felt like a farewell. Sometimes he disappeared for nights at a time. Came home reeking of alcohol, with lipstick he couldn't explain.

The child was born in a hospital run by French nuns. A boy. Linh didn't cry.
Rajesh tried to hold him, but his hands trembled too much.

They gave the baby away two days later, to a French couple from Marseille. Linh didn't look as they left.

25

"He'll have a life we could never give him," she said.

But that night, Rajesh heard her whisper the child's name in her sleep.
And he never answered.

He had started working in a textile factory. She washed dishes. They managed to rent a small room – cold, but together.

Every April, they lit incense for Saigon. Not for the place, but for what it had given them.

One winter, a letter came. His mother was ill.

"You should go," Linh said.
"You're coming with me."

"Your family won't understand me."

"They don't even understand me."

They traveled together. She cared for his mother like a daughter. At the funeral, a cousin asked who Linh was. Rajesh replied:

"My wife."

They remained in India as time passed.

Part VIII: The Lost Years

India, 1991–1999

After his mother's death, India had become their exile within exile. They opened a small fabric studio. Linh did hand embroidery. Rajesh started drinking again. It began discreetly—a glass at dusk. Then two. Then bottles hidden behind rolls of fabric.

He lost himself in younger women. The girls called him Grandpa until the money appeared, then they called him loverboy. He told himself it didn't mean anything. That it was just his body crying out for something Linh no longer gave. But every time he crept home smelling of perfume and whisky, she looked at him as if she already knew.

They never spoke of it. Instead, they sewed in silence beside each other—like two seams in a fabric that never quite matched.

One evening, he found her holding an old photograph—the child. The little boy from Bangkok. She had kept it hidden in an envelope all these years. The photo had been taken by the nuns right after he was born.

"He must be grown now," she whispered.

Rajesh couldn't answer. He walked down to the river and vomited until only bile remained.

When he returned home, she was still awake.

"I want you to stop," she said. "The drinking. The girls. I want to remember you the way you were in Saigon."

He looked at her. And for the first time in a long while, he saw himself too.

The next day, he poured out all the bottles. He sewed with her every evening. And every year in April, they lit three incense sticks: one for Saigon. One for the child. And one for the life that had almost been lost.

Part IX: The Last Scent

Surat, 2008

Rajesh 70. Linh 67.

She grew quieter. One morning, she was sitting in the garden and said,

"I dreamed of Saigon. You were standing on the other side of the river. I couldn't reach you."

"I'm always waiting," he said.

A week later, he found her sleeping forever in the studio. The neighborhood children placed white flowers on her grave.

He began writing letters to her every night:

"You lay in the rain in Saigon and smiled."

"Today the jasmine bloomed."

"I heard someone playing the piano. It sounded like you."

One evening, he closed his eyes in the courtyard. The jasmine smelled strong. A breeze swept through the garden, like a whisper:

Farewell, my beauty.

Part X: The Silence of Blood

Surat, winter 2015

The mail lay as usual in a careless pile by the threshold. Rajesh, now frailer, with thicker glasses and a thinner voice, picked up the envelopes with trembling fingers. Electric bill. Advertisements. A letter from Bombay. Sender: Arjun Moreau. The name meant nothing to him.

He opened it slowly, the way one does with something they already sense is too late.

Mr. Patel,

My name is Arjun. I was born in Bangkok in 1975 and adopted by a French family. I recently took a DNA test through an international database. A match led to your name. It says you are my biological father.

Rajesh sat down slowly. His heart beat unevenly. He read the letter three times. Each time, the letters grew heavier. He struggled to breathe. Tears began to stream down his cheeks.

I'm not seeking answers—only presence. I will come to Surat next month. If you don't wish to meet, I will understand.

The day before Arjun arrived, Rajesh went to Linh's grave. He hadn't been in a long time.
He carried a sprig of jasmine in his pocket, picked from their fading garden.

"He's coming tomorrow," he said softly.
"Our son."

The earth gave no reply.

But the wind lifted a few leaves—like a wink.

Surat, the next day

Arjun was tall, lighter-skinned than Rajesh, with eyes that resembled Linh's—dark, sorrowful, watchful. He stood in the doorway, looking like someone who had traveled far without ever quite arriving.

They sat across from each other at the kitchen table. The tea grew cold between them.

"I've thought about you my whole life," Arjun said at last. "Not as who you were. Just… that you existed."

Rajesh swallowed. "We did what we thought was best. We had nothing. Not even each other."

"I'm not here to judge," Arjun said.

He took an old photo from his pocket. It was faded, almost translucent. A woman with narrow eyes and a tired smile—Linh.

"Is that…?"

Rajesh nodded. "Your mother. She placed that photo in your gown before the nuns took you away."

They sat in silence for a while. Then Rajesh stood and fetched a box from the wardrobe. Inside was a letter he had never dared to send, written to: My son, if you ever look for me…

He handed it over with both hands.

"Would you like to stay the night?" he asked.

Arjun looked at him, his eyes glassy.

"I'll stay as long as you need me."

Part XI: The Final Moment

Surat, Spring 2017

Time no longer flowed—it dropped, slowly, still, like an hourglass made of ash.

Rajesh was tired now. Not sick in any way doctors could name—just tired in his soul. He spent most of his time lying in his wicker chair on the veranda, a blanket over his legs and Arjun sitting beside him, sometimes quietly reading, sometimes just there.

Every evening, Arjun watered the jasmine in the garden. It had bloomed again—for the first time in many years.

One night, when the moon hung low and the air smelled like childhood and regret, Rajesh whispered:

"I think… I've come home now."

Arjun looked at him. "What do you mean?"

"I searched for her in every woman. For myself in every city. For the future at the bottom of a bottle. But what I needed… it was already inside me."

He took Arjun's hand.

"I never thought you'd come. And when you did… everything fell into place."

Arjun said nothing. He just held the old man's hands, gently stroking the skin that had grown thin as rice paper.

Later that night, Rajesh awoke to a scent.

Jasmine.

It wasn't just from the garden. It was stronger—alive, warm. He opened his eyes—and there, in the doorway, stood Linh.

She looked just as she had in Saigon. Dark hair, white dress, hands folded in her lap.

"You came back," he whispered.

"I never left you."

She reached out her hand.

And Rajesh smiled. For the first time in a long while, he smiled like a young man.
Like someone who knew he had been forgiven.

He closed his eyes, took her hand—and exhaled.

Part XII: Epilogue

Arjun buried him next to Linh, beneath the jasmine tree they had planted together. On the grave, he placed two items: a piece of fabric from Surat and a piano-shaped ivory pendant he had found among his mother's belongings.

Every April, he lit three incense sticks.

One for Saigon.

One for love that had survived everything.

And one for a father who had finally come home.

© 2025 Huynh Tan Hung

Publisher: BoD · Books on Demand, Östermalmstorg 1,

114 42 Stockholm, Sverige, bod@bod.se

Print: Libri Plureos GmbH, Friedensallee 273,

22763 Hamburg, Tyskland

ISBN: 978-91-8097-061-7